X

MARIE CURIE

Po
Ra

MARIE CURIE

LEONARD EVERETT FISHER

MACMILLAN PUBLISHING COMPANY
New York

Maxwell Macmillan Canada   Toronto

Maxwell Macmillan International   New York   Oxford   Singapore   Sydney

CHRONOLOGY OF MARIE SKLODOWSKA CURIE

1867 .... Born Marya Sklodowska in Warsaw, Poland

1876 .... Oldest sister, Zosia, dies of typhus

1878 .... Mother dies of tuberculosis

1885–1889 ...... Works as a governess for two Polish families

1891 .... Becomes a student at the Sorbonne, Paris, France

1894 .... Does study on the magnetic properties of steel
Meets Pierre Curie

1895 .... Marries Pierre at Sceaux

1896 .... Becomes interested in glowing rays seen in uranium ore by Antoine Henri Becquerel

1897 .... Begins work on nature of uranium rays as subject of doctoral thesis
Coins the term *radioactivity*
Daughter Irène is born

1898 .... Joined by Pierre in uranium ray experiments
With Pierre, announces existence of polonium and radium

1900–1906 ...... Teaches physics at Sèvres Higher Normal School for Girls

1902 .... Isolates pure radium for the first time
Father dies

1903 .... Awarded doctor of physical science degree, University of Paris
Shares the Nobel Prize in physics with Pierre Curie and Antoine Henri Becquerel

1904 .... Pierre appointed professor at the Sorbonne
Daughter Eve is born

1906 .... Pierre killed in an accident
Takes Pierre's place at the Sorbonne as assistant professor

1908 .... Appointed full professor at the Sorbonne

1911 .... Awarded Nobel Prize in chemistry

1912 .... Institute of Radium founded in Paris on her behalf

1913 .... Laboratory opened in Warsaw, Poland, in her honor

1914–1918 ...... Helps treat wounded soldiers

1921, 1929 ...... Visits the United States

1922 .... Elected to the French Academy of Medicine

1925 .... Lays cornerstone for Radium Institute of Warsaw

1934 .... Dies of radiation poisoning in Sancellemoz, France

With appreciation to Dr. Graeme Luke,
Professor of Physics, Columbia University

Library of Congress Cataloging-in-Publication Data
Fisher, Leonard Everett. Marie Curie / Leonard Everett Fisher —
1st ed.   p.   cm.   ISBN 0-02-735375-3
1. Curie, Marie, 1867–1934 —Juvenile literature. 2. Chemists—Poland—Biography—Juvenile literature. [1. Curie, Marie, 1867–1934. 2. Chemists. 3. Women—Biography.] I. Title.
QD22.C8F57   1994   93-40211   540'.92—dc20   [B]
Summary: The story of the scientist who, with her husband, discovered radium and, like the other subjects of this picture book series, changed the world.

EUROPE

To my grandson, Gregory Byron
Bienvenue à l'univers, avec l'amour

NORWAY

Stockholm

SWEDEN

DENMARK

Baltic Sea

North Sea

POLAND

Warsaw ■

AIN

THE
NETHERLANDS

Dover

BELGIUM

GERMANY

CZECH
REPUBLIC

SLOVAKIA

èvres
■ Paris
·Sceaux

FRANCE

AUSTRIA

HUNGARY

SWITZERLAND

SLOVENIA

Sancellemoz ·

Adriatic Sea

ITALY

0 20 40 60 80 100 miles

Ligurian Sea

Born Marya Sklodowska in Warsaw, Poland, she became known the world over as Marie Curie—Madame Curie—the frail Polish-French scientist whose work put humanity on a new scientific course.

"Manya," as she was called, was the youngest of five children. They were Zosia, Bronya, and Hela, her sisters, and Jozio, their brother. Neither Zosia, who contracted typhus, nor her mother, Bronislawa, lived past Manya's eleventh birthday.

The Sklodowskis were members of the minor Polish nobility. Vladislav, Manya's father, was a professor of mathematics and physics. Her mother ran a school for girls until her untimely death from tuberculosis. They struggled under the crushing yoke of the Russian tsars who ruled them. To the Sklodowskis, books meant more than the lands their ancestors once owned. They believed that learning was the most exalted goal in anyone's life, and that learning would keep alive Poland's intellect and restore her independence.

Ten-year-old Manya was the brightest student in Warsaw's Pension Sikorska, a private school for girls. It was Manya who saved her classmates, teacher Antonina Tupalska—"Tupsia"— and the director, Mademoiselle Sikorska, from Siberian exile when the school inspector made one of his surprise visits.

Suspicious Inspector Hornberg fell upon the school, hoping to catch the students studying Polish history and speaking Polish, which were forbidden by the tsar. When the inspector arrived, the children hid their Polish books and sat in wooden silence. Hornberg demanded answers to his questions about Russian history. Manya, her nervousness masked by steely gray eyes, raised her hand and responded correctly in perfect Russian. She could have responded in German, English, or French, too.

Hornberg could not prove that Mademoiselle Sikorska's girls were speaking Polish, which they were, or that Tupsia was teaching Polish history, which she most certainly was!

Between 1885 and 1889, Manya worked as a governess. She hoped to study physics at the University of Paris, at the Sorbonne, the most distinguished school of science in the world. But she sent most of her earnings to Bronya and her husband, Casimir Dluski, who were medical students in Paris.

Manya began attending a physics class in Warsaw's Museum of Industry and Agriculture. The museum was a cover for students, including Manya, who plotted against the Russians.

But Manya realized that her dream of studying in Paris over-whelmed her Polish loyalties. In September 1891, with meager savings and the blessings of her father, Manya packed her clothes, mattress, and bed quilt, and temporarily moved into the Dluskis' Paris apartment. Two months later, having passed the exams, she registered as *Marie* Sklodowska and became a student of physics at the Sorbonne.

For the next three years, Marie sat in the front row of a large lecture hall and listened as great men of science spoke. She was the first and only woman at the Sorbonne. She had few friends.

Eventually Marie lived in a tiny, bare attic room. There she studied in wretched poverty, freezing in the winter, broiling in the summer. Thin and exhausted from lack of sleep, a poor diet, and long hours of study, she was near collapse most of the time. Only her sister Bronya, her youth, and a stubborn desire to succeed saved her.

In 1894, twenty-seven-year-old Marie, a student with a brilliant reputation, was hired to do a study of the magnetic properties of steel. Since she had no laboratory in which to conduct her research, a Polish friend introduced her to Pierre Curie, who managed one.

A tall, soft-spoken, Paris-born physicist eight years older than Marie, Pierre was a noted scientist, as was his brother, Jacques. Pierre was dedicated to pure scientific research. He refused all the honors and money that could have been his, including induction into France's Legion of Honor. In so doing, he earned the hostility of many colleagues—and the admiration of Marie Sklodowska.

Pierre gave Marie a small work space. They spent every spare minute together, discussing science. A year later, in Sceaux, a small country town outside of Paris that was the home of Pierre's parents, Dr. Eugène and Sophie Curie, Pierre and Marie were married.

In 1896, Antoine Henri Becquerel, a French physicist, saw an unusually strong glow in a brown lump of uranium ore called *pitchblende*. There was no light present to cause the glow. And the lump had left a negative image on a photographic plate. A year before, German physicist Wilhelm Konrad Roentgen had discovered X rays—rays of unknown origin that could penetrate a solid material and photographically reveal what was behind or inside it. The glow in the pitchblende struck Becquerel as somehow related to X rays.

Becquerel suggested to the Curies that they look into the mystery. Pierre, busy with his own experiments, urged Marie to make it the subject of her doctoral degree.

Marie began testing chemical elements to identify the substance causing the glow. Her experiments were interrupted in September 1897, when she gave birth to her first child, her daughter Irène. But Marie was soon back in the laboratory, and by the end of the year she had concluded that the mysterious substance was an unknown "radiant" element.

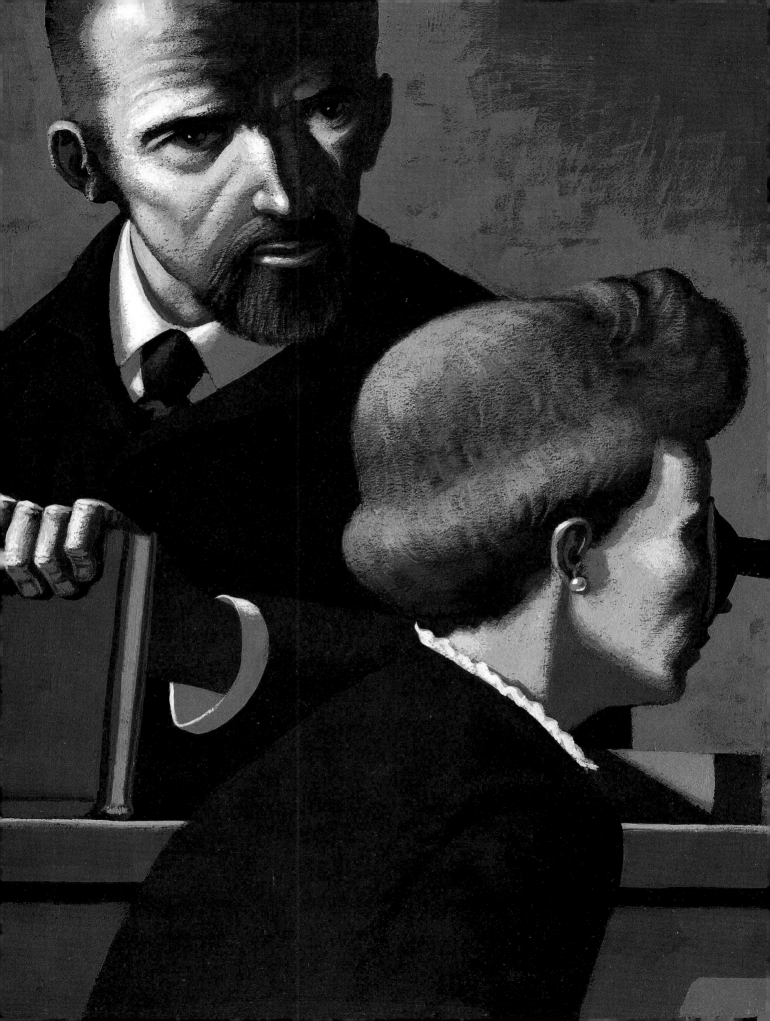

Marie, now aided by Pierre, was on the verge of a great discovery. She brought new terms into the language of science when she characterized this unknown substance as a *radioelement,* or as being *radioactive.* What Marie described was an element having an unstable atomic core, or nucleus, which could disintegrate, producing energy that glowed. A nuclear reaction! Marie was confident that an undiscovered radioactive element was imprisoned in the pitchblende.

She and Pierre announced the discovery of this new element in July 1898. Marie named it *polonium* for her native country, Poland. But there was something more powerful still trapped in the pitchblende. Later that year, on December 26, the Curies announced the existence of a second element, more highly radioactive than any other known. They called it *radium.*

If radium did exist, then long-held ideas about the nature of matter would no longer be acceptable. Before scientists would allow the Curies to rewrite nature's laws, they needed proof. They needed to see this new element.

Over the next four years, with Pierre's help and that of Petit, an assistant, Marie stubbornly labored in an old, leaky shed whose dampness gave Pierre painful rheumatism. Marie, smarting from radiation burns, ached from mysterious ailments that came and went. All the while, she continued to teach physics at a Sèvres school for girls outside of Paris and used some of her wages to help relatives and needy students.

Finally, in 1902, the year in which her father died, Marie produced one-tenth of a gram of pure radium from a ton of pitchblende. The amount was like a teardrop in the ocean. Yet its glow was a million times stronger than that of uranium rays. What awesome power lay in the atomic structure of that element! (Polonium turned out to be a relative of radium, which, as it decayed, usually changed into another element, lead.)

On June 25, 1903, having submitted her paper "Researches on Radioactive Substances," Madame Sklodowska Curie was formally awarded her doctor of physical science degree.

ALFR·
NOBEL

NA
MDCCC
XXXIII
OB
MDCCC
XCVI

In November 1903, the Nobel Prize in physics, one of the most important awards in the world, was given to Antoine Henri Becquerel and to Pierre and Marie Curie for their work on uranium and radioactivity. The Curies did not attend the ceremony in Stockholm. Marie was recovering from one of her frequent ailments, and Pierre begged off, claiming teaching commitments and poor health. But they did accept the large sum of money that came with the prize. The money enabled Pierre to take a rest from teaching to spare his health, and allowed them both to continue their work without interruption.

The following year, 1904, Marie gave birth to a second daughter, Eve. Pierre was appointed full professor at the Sorbonne and given a laboratory with three assistants. One was Marie, the only celebrated woman of science in the world, who, having isolated pure radium practically single-handedly, had brought the Nobel Prize in physics to France. She was given the job of Pierre's "chief of laboratory work."

In April 1906, Pierre fell under the wheels of a horse-drawn wagon on a rain-soaked Paris street and was instantly killed. Marie, numb with grief, replaced him at the Sorbonne. But she was not given Pierre's rank of full professor, only that of assistant professor. Still, she was the first woman ever to teach at the Sorbonne.

Marie continued to work on radioactive elements but had to give up her Sèvres teaching position. Two years later, in 1908, she was promoted to full professor, becoming the first woman to hold such high rank in the scientific world.

In 1911, Marie was proposed for membership in the French Academy of Science. She was rejected. "Women cannot be part of the Institute of France," one member insisted. Later that year, she was awarded the Nobel Prize in chemistry for the discovery and isolation of polonium and radium. It was the first time anyone had received the Nobel Prize twice, and for two different sciences—first physics, then chemistry. Marie's only wish was to see her work—and Pierre's—used to improve the human condition, especially to cure cancer. It was her hope that by exposing diseased tissue to controlled radium rays, illnesses such as cancer would be conquered.

A year later, in 1912, the Institute of Radium was founded in Paris to enable Marie to continue researching the radium-based science of radiology.

In 1913, while the institute was being built, Marie traveled to Warsaw to dedicate a laboratory established in her honor. Defying the Russians who ruled Poland, she delivered her lecture in Polish, still the forbidden language.

The Institute of Radium opened in 1914. Technicians and students came to the institute from around the world. Among them were young Poles whose expenses were secretly paid by Marie.

In 1914, Europe exploded in a world war. Marie took Irène to the battlefields of France in a truck loaded with X-ray and radium therapy equipment. With Marie driving, they visited frontline hospitals. There they set up their machines to locate shrapnel embedded in the torn flesh of thousands of soldiers and to heal the gaping wounds. Marie and Irène saved lives. They also taught American and British allies how to use the equipment.

When the war ended in 1918, many noncombatants, including Irène, were decorated by the French government for their heroic wartime roles. But not Marie. Rumors persisted that before the war Marie had had an unproven love affair that offended powerful people. Marie Curie, who had been and would be decorated by nearly every government in the world, was ignored by victorious France for her battlefield contributions. The Soldier's Cross of the Legion of Honor was the only medal she really wanted. Because she was denied it, she refused later to allow the Legion of Honor to admit her as a member.

In 1922, Marie Curie was elected to the French Academy of Medicine for her contributions to radiological medicine. She was the only woman thus recognized.

"We salute you, a great scientist . . . a patriot, who in war as in peace, has always done more than her duty," read the citation.

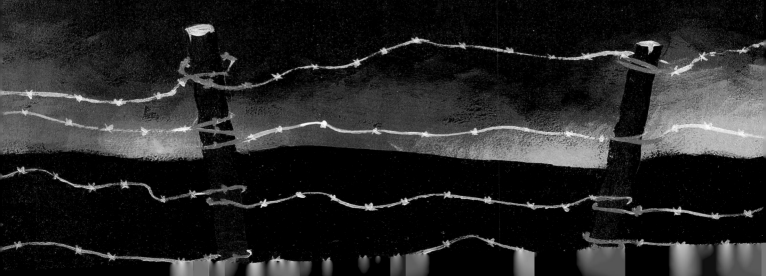

In 1921, and again in 1929, an ailing, exhausted Marie Curie visited the United States. She was wined, dined, and honored by almost every notable American institution and personage, including presidents Warren G. Harding and Herbert C. Hoover. Marie was given a gram of radium worth $100,000, which had been purchased through a national campaign set up by a committee of wealthy women. Admirers gave her money. While she was in the United States, some American scientists and university officials complained loudly that too many dollars were being delivered to foreign scientists. Some of her critics claimed that Marie Curie had done nothing of importance since Pierre's death.

In 1925, she returned to Warsaw, now the capital of Poland, a free and independent nation since 1918, to lay the cornerstone of the Radium Institute of Warsaw.

Nine years later, plagued by a variety of ailments that she herself suspected were the result of exposure to radium, Marie Sklodowska Curie died of radiation poisoning. Her aches and pains were no longer a mystery.

MORE ABOUT MARIE CURIE

In 1912, while recovering from one of her spells of exhaustion, Marie became friends with Albert Einstein. The younger Einstein was celebrated for theories he had put forward in 1905 that would lead to the splitting of the atom and to the atom bomb.

The Curies, Marie and Pierre, revolutionized modern science and opened wide the door to the study of the atom, ushering in the nuclear age. But it was Marie's stubborn effort that changed the knowledge base of science, leading to additional discoveries such as radon, a decayed form of radium. As for radium itself, it is still a rare and precious element that has been widely used in the cure of some forms of cancer and skin disease.

Marie Curie never profited commercially from her work for fear that this would taint the pure research to which she was dedicated. In 1923, the French Academy of Science, which had elected Pierre Curie a member but rejected Marie, celebrated the twenty-fifth anniversary of the discovery of radium. On that occasion, the president of France, Alexandre Millerand, offered Polish émigré Marie Sklodowska Curie a pension, to be inherited by her French-born children, as a "feeble but sincere witness of the universal sentiment of enthusiasm, respect, and gratitude." The agreement was signed by every representative of France, every member of the French government, and every member of the French Parliament.